A Tooth Story

For Jamie McElhiney and Kate McElhiney,
and their reluctant teeth
—M. M.

SIMON SPOTLIGHT
An imprint of Simon & Schuster Children's Publishing Division
1230 Avenue of the Americas, New York, NY 10020
This Simon Spotlight edition August 2021
First Aladdin Paperbacks edition July 2004
Text copyright © 2004 by Simon & Schuster, Inc.
Illustrations copyright © 2004 by Mike Gordon
SIMON SPOTLIGHT, READY-TO-READ, and colophon are registered
trademarks of Simon & Schuster, Inc.
For information about special discounts for bulk purchases, please contact Simon &
Schuster Special Sales at 1-866-506-1949 or business@simonandschuster.com.
Manufactured in the United States of America 0721 LAK
2 4 6 8 10 9 7 5 3 1
Cataloging-in-Publication Data was previously supplied for
the paperback edition of this title from the Library of Congress.
Library of Congress Cataloging-in-Publication Data
McNamara, Margaret. A tooth story / Margaret McNamara ; illustrated by Mike Gordon.
p. cm.—(Ready-to-read) (Robin Hill School) Summary: Jamie longs to have at least one
tooth missing in his first-grade class picture, just like his friends, and when picture day
arrives an unexpected event gives Jamie his wish. [1. Teeth—Fiction. 2. Schools—Fiction.]
I. Gordon, Mike, ill. II. Title. III. Series. PZ7.M232518Tr 2004 [E]—dc22 2003011903
ISBN 978-1-5344-9525-8 (hc) ISBN 978-0-689-86423-0 (pbk)

A Tooth Story

written by Margaret McNamara
illustrated by Mike Gordon

Ready-to-Read

Simon Spotlight
New York   London   Toronto   Sydney   New Delhi

It was almost
school picture day
at Robin Hill School.

"There will be many
empty spaces in
our picture,"
said Mrs. Connor.
"Look at the Tooth Chart."

The Tooth Chart
showed how many teeth
the first graders had lost.

7

Emma had lost three teeth.
Reza had lost four teeth.

TOOTH CHART

Hannah	O		Nick	O
Emma	O O O		Eigen	O O O
Michael	O O		Megan	O O
Reza	O O O O		Griffin	O O
Ayanna	O O O O O O			
Katie	O O			
Mia	O O			
Neil	O O O			

Ayanna had lost six teeth.

But Jamie had lost
no teeth at all.

"Who cares?" said Jamie.
"Who cares about teeth?"

But Jamie did care.

Every night,
he looked in the mirror.

He wiggled his teeth.

They were loose.

They were wobbly.

But they did not come out.

Jamie's mother said,
"I am happy that you will
have a nice, toothy smile
for your class picture."

"I guess I am happy too,"
Jamie said.

The next day
was picture day.

Everything was fine
until they went outside
for recess.
Then . . .

Nick chased a ball.

Emma chased Nick.

Katie ran into Emma.

And Jamie ended up
under them all.
"Ouch!" cried Jamie.

Jamie went to the nurse.
The nurse looked at Jamie.

"I have news," she said.

"You have lost something."

"Did I lose a tooth?"
asked Jamie.
"No," said the nurse.
"You lost two teeth."

Jamie added his name
to the Tooth Chart.

TOOTH CHART

Hannah O   Nick   O

Emma   O O O   Eigen   O O O

Michael O O   Megan   O O

Reza   O O O O   Griffin O O

Ayanna O O O O O O Jamie   O O

Katie   O O

Mia   O O

Neil   O

Then the first graders
had their class picture
taken.

There were many
empty spaces,
just as Mrs. Connor had said.

Jamie took his picture home
a few days later.
"Look, Mom!"
he said.

"I like your smile,"
said his mother.
"It is not toothy,"
said Jamie.
"But it is very,
very happy."